WEDDING GIFTS

A Glimmer Vale Chronicles Story

MICHAEL KINGSWOOD

ABOUT THIS BOOK

It's three hours until the wedding of Raedrick Baletier to Lani Millens, and Melanie Klemins doesn't have a present for them.

Or rather, she did. But she lost it.

Now it's up to Julian Hinderbrook to find the gift and retrieve it, or the wedding will be ruined and the couple's magical day tarnished forever.

Wedding Gifts is a short story set between Books 4 and 5 of the Glimmer Vale Chronicles.

Enjoy the book! After you're done, please come to Michael's website and sign up for his mailing list at michaelkingswood.com/newsletter-signup/. Guaranteed to be spam free, he uses it to announce new releases and special promotions for his fans.

MAP OF GLIMMER VALE

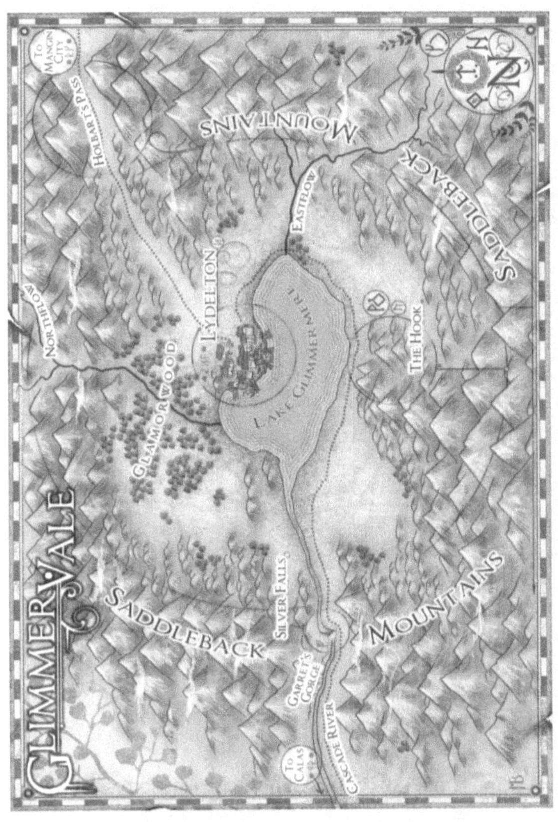

WEDDING GIFTS

"Julian, I need your help."

Julian Hinderbrook put down his tankard and turned in his chair to look at the speaker.

He knew it was Melanie before he saw her. No other woman had her relatively deep voice and refined manner of speech, not in Lydelton at least. And no one else had that way of making a request seem a command. Though, truth to tell, he and his fellow Constable, Raedrick Baletier, had come to her requesting help far more often than she had come to them.

It was full Spring now in Glimmer Vale, and the townsfolk of Lydelton had removed their winter layers eagerly. Melanie was no exception this day, wearing a simple but elegant deep blue gown that was laced at the cuffs, hem, and neckline with silver-white thread. A similarly stitched belt cinched the gown in at her waist, accentuating as always the curve of her hips even as it supported the knife she always seemed to wear.

She was a sight to see, between that lush figure, the wavy dark brown hair that hung to just past her shoulders, and the blue eyes that flashed with intelligence and could just draw a man in if he was not careful. Ordinarily, Julian would be forced to take a moment to admire her beauty, but the worried expression on her face gave him pause.

"What do you need?" He gestured at the empty chair at his table.

Melanie sat, but paused to glance over her shoulder toward where Molli Millens stood over by the bar that ran most of the length of the other side of the taproom from Julian's table. The Oarlock's proprietor, and mother of the bride-to-be, was dressed in her usual flowery dress covered by a white apron, and she beamed with happiness as she chivvied her similarly-aproned barmaids around in their efforts to ready the taproom of The Oarlock for the night's festivities.

Molli had gone all out for it. Flowers of all sorts were strung up on lines that spanned the width of the taproom, and the bar had been scrubbed until the darkly-stained wood of its countertop gleamed in the sunlight that spilled in through the open windows at the front of the room. The two fireplaces, opposite each other near the front, were clear of ashes and soot stains, filled instead with more flowers in pots. The small stage that she set up most evenings for performances was draped in a white cloth, with a polished steel trellis center-stage where the high priest would give his blessings.

And of course it wouldn't be Molli Millens' place without a mouth-watering blend of scents pouring out from the kitchens at the rear. Spiced fish, fried potatoes, and stewed beef overlaid a veritable cornucopia of goodness that made Julian wish he hadn't just finished lunch.

"Have you gotten a gift for Raedrick and Lani yet?"

Melanie's question drew Julian's attention back to

her, and he blinked. That was not the sort of question he expected. "Uh... Yes, why? Haven't you?"

Melanie flushed slightly.

He could only stare in disbelief. "Melanie, the wedding's in three hours!"

The flush increased, but the level look Melanie directed at him was more irritated than embarrassed. "I am well aware of that. It's - "

One of the few barmaids that Molli let get about her normal duties today arrived right then, and Melanie clamped her mouth shut in a little scowl.

"Get you something, Mistress Klemins?" the girl, a homely blonde just off her mother's purse strings named Telli, said, and actually bobbed a little curtsy.

For a second Julian thought Melanie was going to give Telli the rough side of her tongue, but she visibly pulled her irritation back and shook her head. "No, thank you."

Telli nodded and made another curtsy, then flashed Julian a quick smile before hurrying off to the only other occupied table in the front section of the taproom, where four grey-cloaked fishing men from the night shift were having their dinner in front of one of the fireplaces.

A cleared throat from Melanie prompted Julian to turn away from watching Telli depart. "You were saying?"

"Yes." Melanie drew in a breath. "Lani made Raedrick a new winter cloak, did you know that? With her own two hands."

Julian shook his head. "Wow."

"Indeed. She showed it to me shortly after it was made, and I had an idea. She gave me permission to try, and..." She stopped and fixed him with another one of her trademark level looks. "Do you remember what I told you about magical constructs?"

"Pretty much. You put the components of the spell inside the thing and it can do the spell."

She smirked. "There is a bit more to it than that, but close enough. Anyway, I've been researching these constructs since we tussled with Job and Iben."

Julian couldn't help but scowl at the mention of the two corrupt Royal Marshalls. They had robbed the Covington Brothers' Fishing Company and nearly brought Lydelton's economy to its knees, and only quick action and a bit of magical assistance from Melanie had allowed him and Raedrick to catch them before they could make their escape.

Melanie continued, "I believe I've worked out the trick to it. I resolved to enchant the brooch for Raedrick's new cloak so that it would create heat within the cloak itself."

"You're kidding."

Melanie shook her head. "It seemed so easy, so simple. What could go wrong?"

Oh no. Julian saw where this was going. "You burned up the cloak, didn't you?"

"What? No, of course not!" Melanie looked offended for a second, but then that faded and became full-on embarrassment. She looked away, avoiding Julian's eyes. "No. The cloak...flew away out my window."

Julian just sat there, gaping at her, speechless.

Several seconds passed, then Melanie looked back at him and her irritated scowl returned. "Close your mouth before you swallow a fly."

Instead of doing that, Julian took a long drag on his tankard. He swallowed a mouthful of Molli's signature ale and slowly lowered the tankard back onto his table again, then finally spoke. "The cloak flew away."

Melanie nodded.

"Of its own accord."

Another nod.

He couldn't help it, he burst out in laughter. Oh, that was too rich!

"Julian."

He slapped the table, still laughing, and had to pinch his eyes shut to hold back tears of mirth.

"Julian, this is serious."

He tried to respond, but looking at her steadily deeper flushing cheeks sent another spasm of laughter through him.

"Julian!" She slapped the table herself. Hard, and not out of mirth.

That combined with the ice in her eyes stopped his laughter. Mostly.

He held up a finger, requesting a moment, then took another quick drink. "Well, you *have* got a problem there. What do you need me to do?"

"Find it, of course!"

He blinked innocently at her. "Melanie, I'm the Constable, not a finder of flying cloaks."

"Do you think I would ask you if it wasn't important?" Her voice all of a sudden was a mixture of consternation and near desperation.

Julian looked at her more closely, and realized that she was well and truly upset. Those level looks, the icy stare...those had just been a mask. That tightness around her eyes was genuine fear that she had just ruined Lani's wedding day.

He reached out and laid his hand on her shoulder. Giving it a gentle squeeze, he said. "Don't worry, we'll find it."

Melanie gave a quick shake of her head. "We? No, I said I need *you* to find it."

"Hold on a second here. I'm willing to help, but -"

"I figured out the mistake I made in the enchantment, but I need time to prepare the correction.

Bring the cloak back to my shop in the next hour and a half, and I should be able to fix it in time for the ceremony."

He snorted. "Don't you think it would be best to just leave enchantments alone at this point? Give them a pot or something?"

She looked at him like he was daft.

Finally, after a long several seconds that felt like several minutes, Julian rolled his eyes toward the ceiling and threw his hands up. "Fine. I'll find the doubly-cursed cloak." Draining the last of his tankard, he stood, grabbed up his baldric and scabbard from where it had been leaning against his table, and slipped the baldric over his shoulder. "Don't suppose you know where it is?"

Melanie shook her head. "It flew off to the northwest."

"Great. Well, I'd best get to it then."

Melanie smiled at him.

He turned away from the table and took a step toward The Oarlock's front door.

"Remember. An hour and a half. No longer."

Julian looked back over his shoulder and smirked. "Don't you trust me, Melanie?"

She just gave him a level look in return.

Against his better judgment, he found he was laughing again as he walked out the door.

Julian received no fewer than a dozen quizzical looks from townsfolk as he departed The Oarlock and traversed Lydelton's streets to the west and north, asking if anyone had seen a flying cloak.

The odd looks would have been tolerable, but one older fellow, a retired blacksmith if Julian recalled correctly, asked whether he had taken a blow to the head.

Julian stopped asking after that, just trudged up the paving stones of Main Street, muttering to himself and keeping his eyes raised to the sky, searching for any hint of the cloak. He quickly lost the feeling of amusement he had when he departed The Oarloack and was steadily getting more and more irritated.

It was completely understandable that Melanie would want to experiment with her new discoveries. But now? With this?

Normally she was pretty level-headed. What was she thinking?

He only realized he was scowling when a young lad, running full out from a side street, turned toward him and, seeing his face, turned and ran the other way.

Julian sighed and shook his head at his own silliness. No sense getting in a huff over this. After all, it truly was more amusing than anything else, if he thought about it honestly.

He picked up the pace, continuing down Main Street and looking to and fro.

If I were a flying cloak, where would I hide?

That was the question, and Julian pondered it for two blocks before he came up with a possible answer.

The same place birds do: corners of rooftops, steeples, lamps, things like that.

Stopping, he turned a full circle, carefully examining the buildings in that area of town. Most were low, single or two stories, with sharply pointing roofs designed to allow the heavy snowfall that came during the Vale's winters to slide off easily.

That left some nice nooks and crannies to hide in. But where...?

Ah ha!

Bigsbe's Boarding House, back a street or two from Main Street, though two stories tall itself, was still a fair bit taller than its surrounding neighbors. It had a long roof, and was just about on a direct northwest line from Melanie's Mystical Crafts.

Feeling more cheerful now that he had a target to aim at, Julian turned off of Main Street and its paving stones, and onto the packed earth of Lydelton's side streets. A quick right and then a left, and he stood before the Boarding House's front entrance.

Ok, now what?

He slowly paced the length of the building, squinting upwards at the eaves. It made sense that the cloak might...

There.

Over at the leftmost corner of the building, where the roof abruptly changed direction, something dark was hanging in the eaves. Hanging...like a bat. Except bats weren't out in the open in the middle of the day.

The thing fluttered slightly as the breeze took it, and Julian grinned in triumph.

Got it.

That left just how to get it down. He peered about, but the side street was clear of boxes, carts, or other things he could stand on. The Boarding House's stairs were inside the building, and the corner was far enough from the closest windows that it wouldn't do him any good to try that route.

So, no getting up to it. Maybe he could knock it down. There were any number of small stones lying about on the side of the street.

Worth a shot.

Julian grabbed up a couple, took aim, and let fly.

The first rock missed wide, but his second struck true, right up by the eaves where the cloak presumably was caught.

It fell, drifting slowly down to the ground like a

leaf falling from a tree. Julian grinned and moved quickly to get below it.

And received the shock of his life.

Halfway down, the cloak stretched out taut. Then it rolled over on itself and dove straight at him.

Flummoxed, Julian could only watch in complete shock as the thing engulfed him in its black length. It wrapped him up tight, and for a second it almost felt as though the thing was going to pick him up off the ground. Then it let him go and he fell.

More like it threw him to the ground.

He landed on his backside and bit his tongue hard. He bellowed out a curse and clutched at his hurt mouth while pushing himself up onto his feet again.

Just in time to see the cloak winging its way upwards until it was level with the rooftops. It leveled and paused in midair for a moment, then zoomed off to the west.

"Son of a bitch," Julian breathed.

Then he set off running after it.

The cloak led him a merry chase, out past the outskirts of town and beyond toward the thick pines of the Glamorwood, and the jagged mountains beyond. Several times, Julian was able to get close enough to wing it with another rock, but each time the cloak was only slowed for an extremely short period of time, not enough for him to catch up fully.

It flew ahead of him over the tall grass that grew between Lydelton and the woods, and Julian began to think that he would not ever catch the cursed thing before it reached the forest. And once it reached the woods, the gig would be up.

To hell with that. This was his best friend and partner's wedding present from his bride!

Julian picked up the pace, fairly sprinting up a shallow rise as the cloak seemed to slow briefly.

He approached the summit. The cloak was much closer now. Maybe he could...

He leapt for all he was worth, stretching his arms upwards and forwards. His fingertips brushed the trailing edge of the garment for a heartbeat.

And then it was gone, and he fell flat onto his face on the downslope of the hill. He rolled twice before coming to a halt, then just lay there for a moment, hurting in about a dozen different places.

Overhead, it seemed the cloak actually was mocking him, as it did a slow circle for a few seconds before flying away again, this time more fully west than its previous northwesterly route.

A big chunk of Julian just wanted to stay there, on his back in the grass, and recover for a while.

Not a chance.

He forced himself up onto his feet, then trotted up to the next rise, trying to ignore a twinge in his left knee. At the top, he looked to the west, and blinked in surprise.

A long, low, thatch-roofed building stood there near the edge of the forest: Lydelton's old Ranger Station. Julian hadn't gone near the place in months, and he had almost forgotten it was there. Sure, part of the town's budget went to maintaining it, even though no Rangers were currently stationed there. But that wasn't his and Raedrick's department, and so he had just...not thought about it.

A fluttering black shape veered toward the Ranger Station. The cloak.

Thank the Gods it wasn't heading straight into the woods. If it stopped at the Station...

And sure enough, as it got closer to the building, the cloak dove for its roof.

Curious, that. But Julian wasn't about to let the oddness of the flying cloak's behavior get in the way of his gratitude that it appeared to have stopped moving again.

He hurried down toward the Ranger Station as quickly as he could without making his knee hurt even worse.

When he reached the Ranger Station, he peered closely at its roof and grinned. The black cloak would surely stand out against the yellow-brown of the thatch. It oughtn't take long to find the thing.

And yet, after a complete circuit of the building, he couldn't see it anywhere.

Muttering under his breath, he considered that the cloak may have just ducked down near the Ranger Station, but continued on into the Glamorwood beyond. He glanced up at the sun, beginning its oh-so-brief descent from its zenith to the eastern horizon. He only had a few minutes more to find the cloak or he would miss Melanie's deadline and the gift would be ruined, regardless.

All the same, he had no intention of going into those woods after the damn thing. Not by himself.

So he started to circle back around the building, looking closely up at the rooftop again. And then he saw it.

Up under the overhang, near the peak of the roof, there was a gap between the thatch and the stones that made up the building's wall.

Had the cloak forced itself through that hole?

It seemed inconceivable. But there was no other sign of the garment, and Julian could not very well go back without at least checking to be sure.

There was no way he could fit through that hole, small as it was, and no way to get himself up that high regardless, so Julian proceeded around to the Ranger Station's front door.

He fully expected the door to be locked, and he was not disappointed. Fortunately, the door had an older latch-style knob, and the locks on those were relatively easy to get around.

Julian reached into his belt pouch for the tools he would need, but paused as the inanity of his situation came to the forefront of his mind. He was about to pick the lock on a government building to retrieve a cloak that had been flying on its own through half of town, and which he had been chasing like a lunatic the whole way.

If it hadn't actually happened to him, he never would have believed it.

Shaking his head, Julian chuckled softly and set to work on the lock.

A couple minutes later, the door swung inward on squeaky hinges, and Julian stepped inside.

Within, the Ranger Station was all shadows and dust. Light streamed in through the open door, and more dimly through a pair of windows in the back that were partially covered by curtains. The main room, which took up most of the building's interior, was empty for the most part. Desks, a couple tables, and a collection of chairs sat in a neat stack off to his right. To the left, in the direction of the hole the cloak (hopefully) came in, a single door lead into a squared-off partition that did not reach all the way to the roof. Julian presumed that would have been the Chief Ranger's office.

A thick layer of dust covered everything, and rose in small puffs with each step he took. The place smelled musty, as though it had not been disturbed in years.

And it probably hadn't. The town may have been

keeping the place up, but only the outside, from the look of things.

He moved further into the building and peered about, squinting as he looked for his quarry.

It had to be in here.

He hoped.

A third of the way through a circuit of the main room, he saw it. In the rafters above the Chief's office, again dangling like a bat.

Julian frowned, considering the layout for a moment.

The Chief's Office was squared-off, and looked to have a separate ceiling. If he could get atop it, he could grab the cloak and that would be that.

Blessing the people who left the tables and chairs there, he crossed the room and, after a few minutes' work, had a table moved over next to the office.

Julian rubbed his hands together and got up onto the table, but after stretching up on his tip-toes, he could only get his fingertips atop the wall.

Not enough to pull himself up the rest of the way.

So he went, got a chair, brought it over, and set it on top of the table.

That did the trick. With more huffing and puffing than he would have liked, he was able to hoist himself up far enough to get first his elbows and then a foot up onto the office's ceiling.

And then he was up.

He sat there for a moment to get his breath, and resolved to work on his chin-ups more. Back in his Army days, that little climb would not have been so difficult.

Being Constable was too much of a desk job, apparently.

The cloak hung, unmoving, from the corner rafters a couple paces away. If it knew he was there, it showed no sign.

That thought gave him pause, and he took a second to shake his head, again, at his own foolishness. Of course it didn't know he was there! It was a bloody cloak!

He snorted softly, stepped over, and grabbed it.

As soon as his hand closed over it, the cloak came to life. It detached from the rafters and whipped around wildly, jerking to and fro as if trying to make Julian lose his grip.

Which was absurd, of course. Or maybe not. Melanie hadn't been clear exactly what enchantment she had actually laid upon the thing.

Julian grabbed the flapping end of the cloak with his other hand and pulled it down toward his body.

The garment went wild, twisting in his hands and then flinging itself forward to wrap around Julian's head.

"Son of a bitch!"

He stumbled backwards, loosening his grip on the edges of the cloak and grasping at its main body, trying to loose it from his head.

He couldn't see, and breath was rapidly becoming hard to come by. This would not turn out well if he didn't –

His foot came down on nothing, and Julian tumbled backwards.

A split second later, hard wood struck his back, and then the chair gave way beneath his weight. He continued downward, bouncing off the edge of the table until he landed side-first on the floor.

Julian groaned loudly as his entire back and side screamed at him in protest of the fall. He rolled the rest of the way onto his belly and managed to force the cloak away from his face.

There he lay for a long while, panting with exertion and completely ignoring the futile flapping of the cloak, now pinned between his body and the floor.

Melanie had better know how to fix this stupid thing.

She'd better.

Julian pushed the door to Melanie's Mystical Crafts open and limped inside.

The little bell over the door rang, and Melanie, seated behind the counter on the far side of the room to Julian's left, looked up. Seeing him, her eyes went wide.

"What happened to you?"

Julian scowled. Instead of answering, he hobbled past a cabinet full of charms and a few small pamphlets about spirits and ghosts, or something, toward her.

He unceremoniously dumped the cloak, wrapped up and tied into a ball that had been trying to jump out of his hands the entire way back from the Ranger Station, onto the counter.

The cloak bounced up into the air at once, but Melanie quickly caught it. She studied it for a moment before turning her eyes back on Julian.

"Thank you."

"You're welcome. Now if you'll excuse me, I think I'll go start a fist fight with a giant." He turned back toward the door. "It'd hurt less."

Behind him, Melanie half snorted, half chuckled. "See you at the wedding?"

"Yep."

He left.

An hour later, Julian felt a bit better. His knee still

hurt and his side throbbed, but at least he could walk without looking like a cripple.

But it was worth it, for this.

He stood behind Raedrick and to his right on the stage that Molli used for musical performances in The Oarlock's taproom.

Raedrick was facing his bride-to-be. She wore the traditional white gown, with her blonde hair tied into two braids that hung down over the front of her shoulders onto her chest, and she was radiant. Her mother stood at her side, and for once Molli wasn't wearing an apron.

Raedrick didn't look too bad either, truth be told. He had on his best: a black doublet lined in silver thread that matched the buckle on his sword belt. His boots were polished enough to be almost mirrors. He had trimmed his goatee. Hell, even the strap he used to tie his black hair into a short ponytail glittered in the lamplight.

The High Priest had not been exactly happy to hold the ceremony here instead of the Temple, but he beamed a joyful smile at the many witnesses that occupied the taproom's many chairs and benches.

As the couple said their oaths, Julian looked out at the crowd, and marveled as he always did at how he and Raedrick had managed to go from two guys on the run to respected leaders in the town, even heroes.

Amazing.

"...the gifts?"

The High Priest's words drew Julian's attention back to the couple.

Raedrick smiled and reached into his belt pouch. A collective gasp issued from the mouths of every lady present when he withdrew the necklace he'd procured for this day. It was simple, and truth be told not super expensive. But it was glittery, and when he fastened it around Lani's neck, it set off her deep blue eyes in exactly the right way.

She smiled broadly, then turned to Molli, who retrieved the bundle that contained Raedrick's cloak.

Julian hadn't noticed, when he was struggling with it earlier, just how nice the cloak was. But now, watching Lani drape it over Raedrick's shoulders and fasten the clasp, Julian was impressed. Fine black wool, lined with grey fur and stitched with grey thread at the hems and around the cowl, with a silver brooch on its left breast in the shape of a clenched fist holding a set of scales. Their badge of office as Constables.

It looked as good or better than some garments Julian had seen noblemen wear.

Raedrick appeared taken aback by the gift, even more so when Lani touched the brooch.

The ornament began to glow for a second, turning a faintly reddish hue that quickly dispersed through the cloak itself before fading completely.

Raedrick's eyebrows rose high on his head, and he turned to look out into the audience in Melanie's direction. But very quickly, his attention returned to his bride, and they shared their first kiss as a family.

Julian joined the rest of the crowd in applause.

In between claps, he glanced out to the crowd and found Melanie. Their eyes met and she smiled with obvious satisfaction.

Julian returned the smile in kind.

Thank you for reading my book. I hope you enjoyed reading it as much as I enjoyed writing it.

Every review helps an author out, so whether you loved this book, hated it, or something in between, please take a minute to tell other readers what you thought. All of the online retailers make it very easy to do, and I would really appreciate it.

Feel free to come say hi at my website or on Facebook. I always enjoy hearing from readers, especially since you all are, collectively, my boss.

I also have a weekly podcast, Story Time With Michael Kingswood, where I read stories and talk through some of the latest goings on in my world. I'd love to see you there.

Thanks again. My best to you and yours.

Warm Regards,
Michael Kingswood

MAILING LIST

If you enjoyed this book and would like word on new releases and special deals from Michael Kingswood, sign up for his newsletter on his website. Guaranteed to be spam-free, you can opt out at any time. And you can rest assured he will not share your information with anyone, for any reason.

https://michaelkingswood.com/newsletter-signup/

SUPPORTING PATRONAGE

Michael would like to invite you to become a supporting member of his website. Similar in concept to Patreon, a few dollars a month will give you access to exclusive content, and help him to focus more of his time to writing fun and exciting stories for your enjoyment.

Sign up at his website:

https://www.michaelkingswood.com/membership/supporting-patronage/

Michael Kingswood is 20-year veteran of the US Navy submarine force and a lifelong fan of science fiction and fantasy literature. His work has appeared in numerous collections and anthologies, to include the Fiction River Anthology series from WMG publishing. He holds a bachelors degree in Mechanical Engineering as well as a Master of Engineering Management and a Master of Business Administration. He has four children and currently resides in San Diego.

Find Michael Kingswood online at:

www.michaelkingswood.com

www.facebook.com/michael.kingswood

https://steemit.com/@michaelkingswood

The Champion

Veritas Morte

STORY COLLECTIONS

Tales Of Adventure #1

Tales Of Adventure #2

Short Story 10-Pack

A Jar Of Mixed Treats

SHORT FICTION

Michael has also published a number of shorter works, links
to which can be found on his website.